Greedy Rico

Dedication

This book is inspired by and dedicated to a very special dog named Rico. He loves his food and this short story is an example of his colourful personality.

Once there was a dog called Rico.

Rico was known for being very, very greedy!

He would often scare all the people in the town with his growling bark so they would give him some food.

Every morning, Rico would walk through the town demanding food. All the shopkeepers in the town would hide behind their shop windows when Rico walked by.

"Woof, Woof, Woof!!" Rico said to the baker. The baker had no choice but to give Rico a fresh loaf of bread.

He ate all the bread in only 5 seconds and moved on down the road...

"Woof, Woof, Woof!!" Rico said to the butcher. The butcher had no choice but to give Rico a chunky piece of beef.

He ate all the beef in only 4 seconds and moved on down the road...

"Woof, Woof, Woof!!" Rico said to the grocer. The grocer had no choice but to give Rico a long, fat carrot.

He ate all of the carrot in only 3 seconds and moved on down the road...

"Woof, Woof, Woof!!" Rico said to the fishmonger. The fishmonger had no choice but to give Rico a delicious cut of salmon.

He ate all the salmon in only 2 seconds and moved on down the road...

"Woof, Woof, Woof!!" Rico said to the children playing in the school playground. The children screamed with fear and had no choice but to give Rico their lunches!

He ate all the children's lunches in one big gulp!

When Rico got home he felt very, very sick.

He ate so much food that his stomach felt like it was going to explode!

Rico walked slowly through the town looking for help. But the baker, the butcher, the grocer, the fishmonger and the children had all gone. They had run away from greedy Rico...

Rico decided to stop off at the vet. "Woof!" Rico said to the doctor. The doctor could see Rico was very sick. The doctor said, "I can give you some medicine but you have to promise me you will stop being so greedy and be more friendly towards the people in town".

Rico took the medicine and felt much better.

The next day, Rico walked through the town with a big smile on his face. He stood in the middle of the town and gave one...big..."Woof!"

All the people in the town peeped out of their windows and were shocked!

Rico had the biggest chocolate cake they had ever seen waiting for them.

Everyone rushed outside to have some cake. "This is the most delicious cake I have ever tasted!", said the baker.

Rico wagged his tail with excitement and said, "woof, woof, woof!"

Printed in Great Britain
by Amazon

14942453R00018